HANUKKAH,
OH,
HANUKKAH!

A Treasury of Stories, Songs, and Games to Share

Compiled by Wendy Wax

Illustrated by John Speirs

A Bantam Book

As you read through this book, you will see the word *Hanukkah* spelled in different ways. That's because Hanukkah is a Hebrew word, and the Hebrew alphabet is very different from the English alphabet. So when writers translate this word into English, they use different methods. Some other ways of spelling Hanukkah are: Chanukkah, Hanukah, Chanukah, Hannukah, Channukah, Chanuka.

To Tilly, Siggy, and Alexandra

A PARACHUTE PRESS BOOK

Published by
Bantam Books
a division of
Bantam Doubleday Dell Publishing Group, Inc.
1540 Broadway
New York, NY 10036

Bantam Books are published by Bantam Books, a division of Bantam Doubleday Dell Publishing Group, Inc. Its trademark, consisting of the words "Bantam Books" and the portrayal of a rooster, is Registered in U.S. Patent and Trademark Office and in other countries. Marca Registrada. Bantam Books, 1540 Broadway, New York, New York 10036

ISBN: 0-533-09551-X

Printed in Singapore
October 1993
10 9 8 7 6 5 4 3 2 1

Oh, Hanukkah, Oh, Hanukkah

Contents

Hanukkah Memories to Celebrate

Remembering This Special Hanukkah, 19_____

Place picture here.

The candles were lit by:

_____

_____

_____

_____

Family traditions we keep every Hanukkah:

_____

_____

_____

_____

Place picture here.

Favorite Hanukkah memory:

_____

_____

_____

_____

Oh, Hanukkah, Oh, Hanukkah,
Come light the menorah.
Let's have a party,
We'll all dance the hora.

A Hanukkah Memory by Jack Prelutsky

When I was a boy growing up in the Bronx in the 1940s and 1950s, Hanukkah was a special event for me, and I always looked forward to its arrival. In my family, as soon as I was old enough, my parents let me light the menorah candles and chant the blessings. I was also awarded the same privilege by my synagogue, where I was principal soloist with the congregation's choir.

One year, when I was nine or ten years old, a visitor from a major Jewish organization (I think it was Hadassah) heard me rehearsing with my choir and invited me to perform for her group on the first two nights of Hanukkah. I was to light the candles and sing the blessings in front of thousands of people in the Grand Ballroom of the famous Waldorf-Astoria Hotel in Manhattan.

My parents were working-class people who never had much money, and I knew little of the world outside the Bronx. Except for an occasional trip to Coney Island or an afternoon with relatives in Queens, I'd rarely ventured from my neighborhood....Manhattan seemed as far away as the moon.

It would be an understatement to say I was excited when my mother and I took the subway "downtown" that first night, and by the time we reached the hotel I was practically jumping out of my skin. The ballroom was huge, elegant, brightly lit, and filled with more people than I'd ever seen before. I stood on a platform behind a gigantic menorah, and everyone was looking at me. I was certain I'd forget the words, that my voice would crack, or that some other terrible thing would happen. My voice and hands trembled as I sang and lit the candles....I'm amazed that I didn't pass out. By the time I was finished, my fingers, clean white shirt, and unfashionable tie were covered with melted wax. My mother beamed. It didn't matter to her that her son was covered with paraffin. I was less rattled the second night and dripped only half as much wax.

I must have done a better job than I'd thought, for the same organization invited me back to perform the ceremony the following year at the Belmont Plaza Hotel. I was an old hand by then and got through both nights unwaxed.

In a sense, those Hanukkah celebrations were my introduction to the wider world, and I'm smiling as I write this recollection.

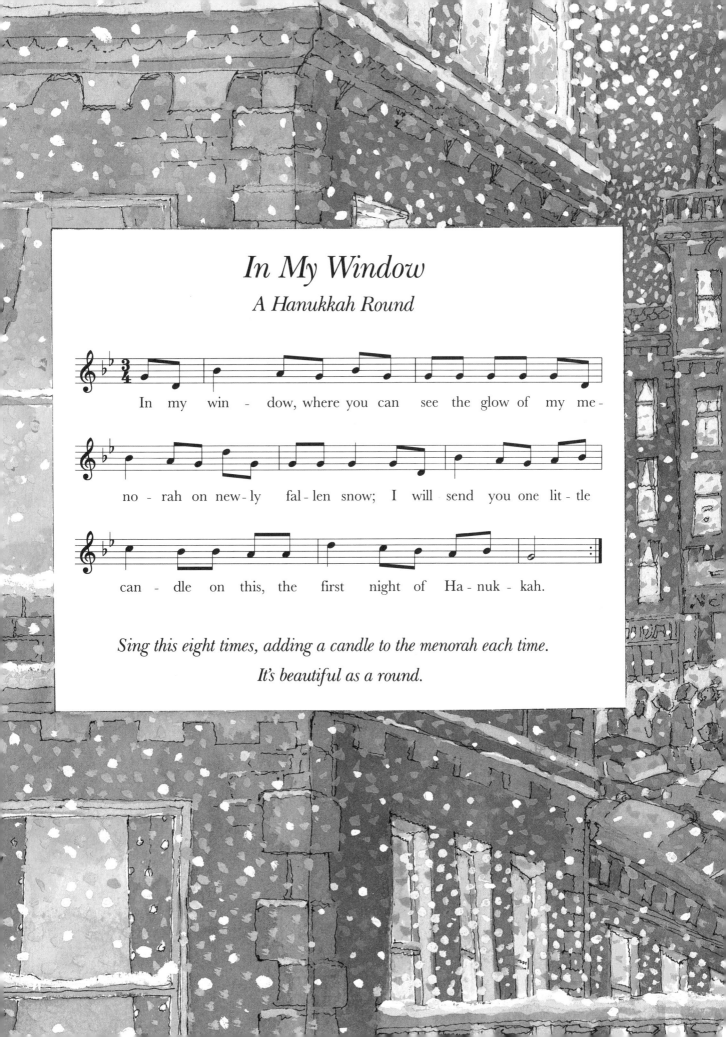

Make a Family Menorah

Start a tradition — make a family menorah. It's easy to do, and everyone in the family can help decorate it. Use your menorah for years to come, or create a new one every year.

You will need:

ten 3/8-inch metal nuts from the hardware store.

These nuts are the perfect size to hold Hanukkah candles.

glue

nine Hanukkah candles

a piece of wood or pasteboard, approximately 5" x 10" x 2"

paint, markers, gold stars, and other decorating materials

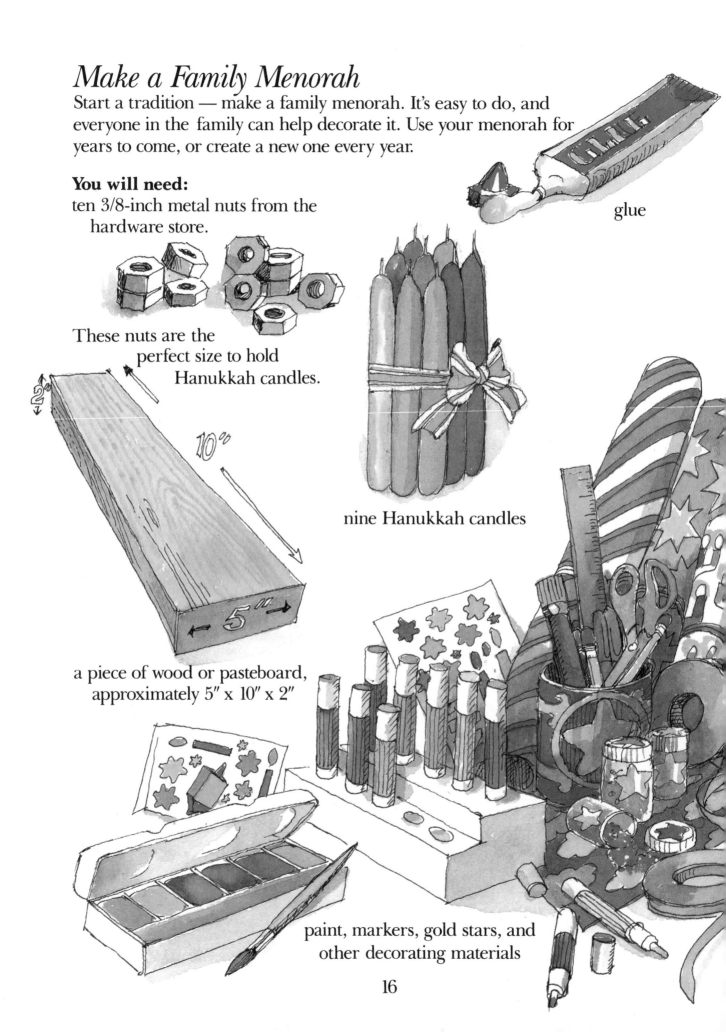

16

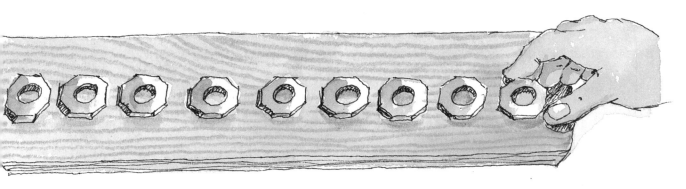

1. Place nine of the nuts in a row on the block of wood.

2. Glue the nuts in place.

3. Take the tenth nut and glue it on top of the middle, or fifth, nut. This will hold the candle called the *shammash*. That's the candle that's used to light the others. The *shammash* will stand taller than the rest.

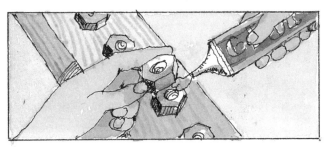

4. Now it's time to decorate the menorah. Every member of the family can help.

Paint the wood.   Draw on it with markers.   Glue on sparkling stars or glitter.

Blessings Over the Hanukkah Lights

Candles are lit after sundown on each of the eight nights of Hanukkah. On the first night a candle is set on the far right side of the menorah. It is lit by the *shammash*, a candle that has its own special setting. On the seven succeeding nights another candle is added from right to left. The candles are kindled by the *shammash* from left to right.

The family member who lights the Hanukkah candles also sings the blessings. When he or she finishes a blessing, everyone else chimes in with "Amen."

Here are three blessings. Sing the first two blessings on each of the eight nights and the last one on the first night only.

First Blessing

Blessed art Thou, O Lord our God, King of the Universe, who has sanctified us by Thy commandments and instructed us to kindle lights of Hanukkah.

1. Ba - rukh A - tah A - do - nai, E - lo - he - nu Me - lekh ha - o - lam,___ a - sher kid - sha - nu be - mitz - vo - tav, ve - tzi - va - nu le - had - lik ___ ner shel ___ Ha - nu - kah.

בָּרוּךְ אַתָּה יְיָ אֱלֹהֵינוּ מֶלֶךְ הָעוֹלָם, אֲשֶׁר קִדְּשָׁנוּ בְּמִצְוֹתָיו
וְצִוָּנוּ לְהַדְלִיק נֵר שֶׁל חֲנֻכָּה.

Second Blessing

Blessed art Thou, O Lord our God, King of the Universe, who has performed miracles for our ancestors in days of old at this season.

2. Ba - rukh   A - tah   A - do - nai   E - lo - he - nu   Me - lekh ha - o - lam,___   she - a - sah ni - sim la - a - vo - te - nu,   ba - ya - mim___   ha - hem   ba - ze - man ha - zeh.

בָּרוּךְ אַתָּה יְיָ אֱלֹהֵינוּ מֶלֶךְ הָעוֹלָם, שֶׁעָשָׂה נִסִים לַאֲבוֹתֵינוּ בַּיָּמִים הָהֵם בַּזְּמַן הַזֶּה.

Third Blessing
Sung on the first night only.

Blessed art Thou, O Lord our God, King of the Universe, who has kept us in life, preserved us, and enabled us to reach this season.

3. Ba - rukh A - tah A - do - nai E - lo - he - nu Me - lekh ha - o - lam,____ she - he - he - ya - nu, ve - ki - ye - ma - nu ve - hi - gi - ya - nu la - ze - man ha - zeh.

בָּרוּךְ אַתָּה יְיָ אֱלֹהֵינוּ מֶלֶךְ הָעוֹלָם, שֶׁהֶחֱיָנוּ וְקִיְּמָנוּ וְהִגִּיעָנוּ לַזְּמַן הַזֶּה.

20

The Lights of Chanukah

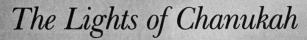

Myra Cohn Livingston

One, our God,
One, our light;
  Chanukah
  Returns tonight.

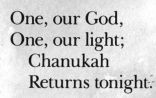

Two, the tablets
Of our law.
  Moses listened.
  Moses saw.

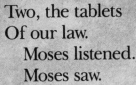
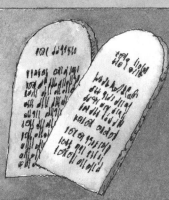

Three, our fathers;
Abraham,
  Isaac, Jacob
  Wise and calm.

Four, the mothers
Of our need;
  Milk and water,
  Bread and seed.

Five, the Books
Our Torah holds;
  Teachings of
  The past unfold.

Six, the days
Of work and play;
  Bricks and mortar,
  Wood and clay.

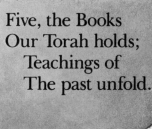

Seven, Sabbath,
  Day of prayer,
  Time of hope
  To ease our care.

Eight, the lights
  Eternally
  Lit for
  Judah Maccabee.

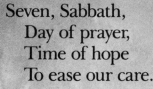

A Festival of Lights
A Selection from More All-of-a-Kind Family
by Sydney Taylor

For generations, young readers have loved the characters that Sydney Taylor created in her popular All-of-a-Kind Family *books. These stories about a Jewish family — Mama and Papa, their five daughters, Ella, Henny, Sarah, Charlotte, and Gertie, and their little son, Charlie — are based on the author's own experiences growing up in a big family at the turn of the century.*

In this excerpt from More All-of-a-Kind Family, *the family celebrates Hanukkah with a party at Aunt Rivka's house. Lots of relatives are there, including Uncle Hyman and his friend from Europe, Lena. It's a wonderful party, and the sisters manage to have more than their share of fun, as you'll soon see.*

Into a dimly lit hallway and up three flights of stairs the family went. Aunt Rivka's tiny boxlike flat was already overflowing with old folks and young. Joyous greetings were exchanged. "Hello, hello!" "Happy Hanukkah!"

Gradually the grownups settled themselves near the big round table while the children were distributed on the couch, laps, assorted stools, and the floor. Someone started a song. With so much fun and laughter, others were encouraged to join. Someone else told a story, and soon the company vied with one another in telling amusing tales.

Aunt Rivka brought in the refreshments. There were high mounds of steaming latkes, fruit, nuts, raisins and dates, and finally her great specialty, rich, brown, moist slices of honey cake. Hot tea was poured into glasses for everyone.

All at once Uncle Solomon slapped his palm on the table. "See, children!" he called out loudly. "See what I have!" He held up a leaden object which looked like a tiny alphabet block with a stem running right through its center. Each of its four sides bore a letter. "A dreidel!

A dreidel!" the children cried.

Uncle Solomon smiled at them through his long white silky beard. "Whoever wants to play with the dreidel must first tell what the letters are."

From various parts of the room there were shouts. "N, G, H, S!"

"That's all right." Uncle Solomon nodded his head. "But who can tell me what they stand for?"

An older boy stood up and recited

in Hebrew, *"Nes Gadol Hayah Sham."*

"That's still all right." Uncle Solomon beamed. "But who knows what the words mean?"

And Ella answered proudly, her voice clear as a bell, "A great miracle happened there."

"Perfect!" Uncle Solomon handed the dreidel to his son. "Here, Nathan, take the children into the kitchen and start them off. Aunt Rivka has the nuts all ready for you."

As the children trooped into the kitchen, there were wails from some of the smaller ones. "But we don't know how to play!"

"I'll teach you," Nathan said good-naturedly. "First, everyone sit down on the floor and make a circle." When everyone had done this, he continued. "Now we divide the nuts evenly amongst us. Then each puts his share in his own saucer. Now each one put a nut in the big bowl here in the center. Now watch." He gave the dreidel a spin. "Let's see what letter comes up. You see, the letters also have a Jewish meaning." The dreidel stopped. "Notice everybody, it's on the N. This stands for *nicht* or nothing. So I take no nuts from the big bowl." He turned to Henny. "Here, you spin next."

Henny gave the dreidel a good hard turn, and it wobbled crazily till it stopped on G. "The G stands for *gantz*, meaning all. You're lucky. You get all the nuts in the bowl."

"But what do we do now, with no nuts left?" a little girl asked.

"Everybody has to put another nut into the bowl," Nathan replied. "Now the next person gets a chance to spin."

They played on. They soon learned that H stands for *halb*, half, which allows the player to take half the nuts from the bowl, and that S stands for *shtell*, or put, which means the player has to add another nut to the pile.

The children enjoyed the game immensely, and the afternoon just flew away. They didn't want to stop playing until Uncle Chaim uttered the magic words "Hanukkah money! Come on, children!"

Thereupon the uncles and aunts made the rounds with a merry jingle of coins. "Happy Hanukkah!" they repeated over and over, as they dropped the precious pennies into open little palms.

And now parents began bundling up their little ones. It had grown late, and the party was at an end. Aunt Rivka and Uncle Chaim stood at the door bidding each one good-bye.

24

Upstairs, as Henny picked up the umbrella, she glanced around the empty front room. It still bore traces of the recent gathering. On the partially cleared table was a large bowl of nuts. "Aunt Rivka," she called out, "can I have some nuts?"

"Why not?" Aunt Rivka shouted back from the kitchen. "Help yourself."

"How many can I take?"

She could hear Aunt Rivka laugh. "Take as much as you can carry."

Oh, boy, exclaimed Henny to herself. All I can carry! Her eyes were alight with sparks of mischief. Carefully she pushed the bowl towards the edge of the table. Pulling back several ribs of the umbrella, she tipped the bowl. In a moment, the nuts were cascading down in a rattle of sound.

As Henny sauntered past the kitchen on her way to the door, she

"May we always meet on happy occasions."

As Uncle Hyman and Lena waved good-bye, Mama suddenly remembered something. "Oh, my! I left my umbrella!"

"I'll get it," Henny volunteered. She started back up the stairs.

"It's in the front room, by the window!" Mama shouted after her. "Ella, you wait for her," she said. "We'll go on ahead. It's way past Charlie's bedtime."

"Mama, can all of us girls wait so we can walk home together?" Sarah asked.

"All right. Ella, see they come right home."

said smoothly, "Thank you, Aunt Rivka. You certainly let me take a lot."

Unsuspecting Aunt Rivka kept right on washing the dishes. "It's all right, my child," she replied, "the more, the merrier."

Henny spluttered with laughter. "Don't you want to see how many you gave me?" she asked mischievously.

Aunt Rivka picked up a towel for her soapy hands and stepped into the front room. When she saw the empty nut bowl, her hands flew up in amazement. "How — why, Henny, you surely can't carry them all!" Henny held up the umbrella in triumph, and Aunt Rivka burst out laughing. "What a girl! Next time I'll know better than to give you such a chance, or I'll find myself with no house left."

"What's the matter with the umbrella?" Gertie asked in amazement as Henny came tramping out of the hallway. "It looks all blown up!"

Henny chuckled. "That's because it's full of something good!"

Charlotte pulled back a rib and peered inside. Her jaw dropped.

"Ooh, nuts! Millions of 'em!"

Three more heads poked themselves inside. "Look out!" Henny yelled. "You'll break Mama's umbrella and spill out all my nuts!"

Ella turned on Henny. "Does Aunt Rivka know about this?"

"Certainly!" Henny countered. "And I was very polite, too. I asked her first."

"Do you expect me to believe that she actually let you have all these?"

Henny grinned. "She said to take as much as I could carry." The grin widened from ear to ear. "So I only did what she told me."

"Mama won't like it," Sarah said immediately. "You know she always says when somebody offers you something, you're supposed to take just a little."

"It's all right. I showed Aunt Rivka how many I had, and she just laughed. I wanted to be sure there was enough for the five of us. Go on," Henny added generously, "help yourselves."

The girls fell to and soon shells were flying in all directions. The way homeward was slow, for every time one picked a butternut, she had to stop and stamp on it with her heel.

After a few blocks Gertie observed, "The umbrella's getting skinnier and skinnier."

Charlotte turned back to stare at the litter of shells strewn behind them. "We're leaving a trail, just like Hansel and Gretel," she said.

By the time they reached their door, they were all full to bursting, and the little ones felt drowsy. "I'm so tired, my mouth is full of yawns," Gertie said.

Sarah stretched her arms wide. "I'm tired too. Didn't we have a good time, though? I wish every day was Hanukkah!"

Let's Dance the Hora

The hora is the dance of happiness. Whether it's danced at a party or at home, the hora is festive and fun for everyone — and best of all, it's easy to learn.

Here's what you do:

Family and friends gather in a circle — the more, the merrier! Then they all place their hands on the shoulders of their neighbors — right hand on the person to the right, left hand on the person to the left. If you can't reach your neighbor's shoulder, hold hands.

Move around the circle by doing the following steps:

1. Step right with your right foot.

2. Put your left foot behind your right foot.

3. Step right again with your right foot.

4. Now hop on your right foot.

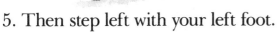

5. Then step left with your left foot.

6. And hop on your left foot.

Repeat these steps over and over. Then switch direction — starting with the left foot and going the other way!

Once the circle's turning, have Grandma and Grandpa step into the center. They can do their own special dance while everyone else dances the hora around them. When Grandma and Grandpa have had enough, it's Mom and Dad's turn. Next come aunts and uncles and then, finally, the children!

A special Hanukkah hora song is on the next page. It's lots of fun to sing while you're dancing.

Mi Yemalel?: Who Can Retell?

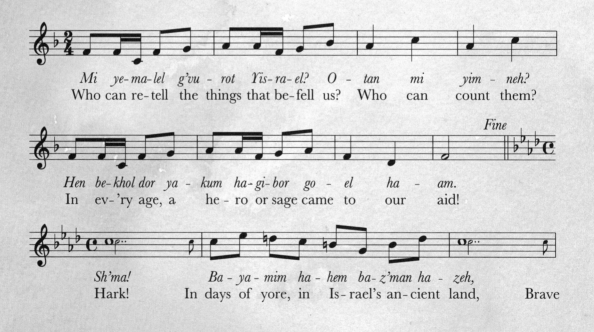

Mi ye-ma-lel g'vu-rot Yis-ra-el? O-tan mi yim-neh?
Who can re-tell the things that be-fell us? Who can count them?

Hen be-khol dor ya-kum ha-gi-bor go-el ha-am.
In ev-'ry age, a he-ro or sage came to our aid!

Sh'ma! *Ba-ya-mim ha-hem ba-z'man ha-zeh,*
Hark! In days of yore, in Is-rael's an-cient land, Brave

Ma - ka - bi   mo - shi - a   u - fo - deh,
Mac - ca - be - us   led   the   faith - ful   band. _____ But

u - v'ya - me - nu   kol   am   Yis - ra - el,
now   all   Is - rael   must   as   one   a - rise, _____ Re-

D.C. al Fine

yit - a - hed   ya - kum   le - hi - ga - el.
deem   it - self through   deed   and   sac - ri - fice.

Gather 'round the table,
We'll give you a treat.
A dreidel to play with
And latkes to eat!

A Hanukkah Memory by David A. Adler

I grew up in a big old house with plenty of room for the eight of us — my parents, my three brothers, my two sisters, and me. Mutti stayed with us too for most weekends and Jewish holidays.

Mutti is German for "Mother," and for us it was fitting that we called her that. She was our grandmother, our mother's mother. But remarkably, virtually everyone who knew her called her Mutti. For many years I didn't know her true first name. It was Alice.

Friends marveled at Mutti's energy. Even in her eighties, she still went regularly to hospitals and nursing homes to visit lonely patients. She called them the "old" people, but most of them were younger than she was.

When Mutti came on Friday for the weekend, for Shabbat, she brought us hand-rolled marzipan, lox wrapped in paper, and often the sort of toys she loved. Among them was a windup plastic chicken that laid a plastic egg and a small bear that walked down a gentle incline.

On Hanukkah, of course, we all played dreidel. Mutti knew the rules of the game, but there was still trouble. My brother Eddie believed in doing things exactly right, and after a few rounds of dreidel he would complain bitterly that Mutti was cheating. I often sat next to her and knew he was right. She did cheat at dreidel — and at most games she played with us. She'd spin a *gimel* and claim it was a *nun*. She'd spin a *heh* and claim it was a *shin*. Mutti didn't need to win. She just wanted her grandchildren to be happy. She cheated so that she would lose and we would win.

What's in My Pocket?

Sadie Rose Weilerstein

Clinkety, clinkety, clinkety, clink!
What's in my pocket? What do you think?
Pennies! A nickel! A quarter! A dime!
Didn't you know it was Hanukkah time?
Nickels, a quarter, a dime, and a penny!
Hanukkah gelt! Have you got any?

Five Little Pieces of Hanukkah Gelt
Fingerplay

I have five little pieces of Hanukkah gelt.

Count on fingers.

The first one said,
"Eat me up before I melt."

The second one said,
"I have gold foil on both my sides."

The third one said,
"Peel it to see where the chocolate hides."

The fourth one said,
"Eat me up fast."

The fifth one said,
"I am the last."

Hanukkah gelt
is so good to eat.
Hanukkah gelt
is my favorite treat!

Malke's Secret Recipe
A Chanukah Story by David A. Adler

In Chelm, as in other towns, each family had its own latke recipe. In some families the recipe had been handed down from mother to daughter for many generations. Some people added just salt and pepper to the potatoes. Others added eggs and onions. There were even people who added paprika, parsley, and bread crumbs.

Most people were happy to share their latke recipes. But not Malke,

the tailor's wife.

"I may be a poor woman," Malke said, "but I make the best latkes in Chelm, and I'm the only one who has the recipe."

When Malke was a young bride, she would let people taste her latkes. She wanted everyone to know how good they were. But Malke became afraid that someone eating her latkes might be able to taste each ingredient and learn her recipe. Since then, she only

let her husband and children eat her famous latkes.

As the years passed, Malke's latkes tasted even better in people's memories than they had tasted on their forks.

Berel, the shoemaker, always closed his eyes and smiled when he remembered Malke's latkes. "They were so very soft," he would tell his wife, Yentel, "and so very light. Eating Malke's latkes was like eating a cloud."

Then one Chanukah night, Berel, Yentel, and their children were eating latkes. These were not soft and light latkes, but thick, heavy ones.

Berel took one bite and banged on the table. "Enough!" he shouted. "I'm tired of the same latkes every Chanukah. Tomorrow I'm getting Malke's recipe."

The next morning Berel told Yentel, "I'm not opening the shop today. If someone comes with his

shoes, tell him to come back tomorrow. But don't tell him where I've gone."

Berel hid behind a tree near Malke's house. He waited there all day, but Malke didn't make latkes.

That night, Berel watched as Malke and her family lit their Chanukah candles. He heard them sing *Maoz Tzur*, "Rock of Ages," and he watched them play dreidel.

Then Berel saw Malke take out some potatoes, a grater, and a large pan.

"This is it!" Berel said to himself. "Tonight I will eat latkes as soft and light as a cloud."

Berel crawled close to the window. He watched and wrote down everything Malke did.

When the latkes were done, Berel ran home to his wife, Yentel.

"I've got it!" he said. "I've got Malke's recipe."

Berel looked at his paper. "First take five potatoes and two eggs," he read.

"Some secret recipe," Yentel said as she watched Berel peel the potatoes. "We always use potatoes and eggs."

Berel grated the potatoes into a bowl. He added the eggs.

"We do that, too," Yentel said.

"Now," Berel read. "Chop six scallions very fine."

"Scallions!" Yentel said. "Who ever heard of using scallions in latkes? Everyone uses an onion. An onion is better."

"So I'll use an onion," Berel said. He chopped it and mixed it in with the potatoes.

"Next," Berel said, "Malke mixed in flour."

"Don't use flour. Use bread crumbs," Yentel said.

Berel used bread crumbs.

Berel added some salt. He looked down at his paper and was about to add pepper when Yentel shook her head and said, "Pepper makes me sneeze."

Berel didn't add the pepper.

"Now I need a lemon," Berel said. "Malke squeezed in a few drops of lemon juice."

Yentel shook her head. "No. Lemon juice belongs in tea."

"And Malke added parsley," Berel continued. "She made her latkes very thin and fried them in vegetable oil."

"Parsley! Vegetable oil! That's not a secret recipe. That's secret nonsense," Yentel said. "Parsley belongs in a salad with carrots. In this house we fry in chicken fat. And thick latkes taste better than thin ones."

Berel and Yentel made their latkes with potatoes, eggs, salt, and bread crumbs, just like they always did. They made their latkes very thick and fried them in chicken fat.

When the latkes were done, Berel and Yentel and their children sat down to eat them. They ate slowly. They wanted to know if Malke's latkes really did taste better than anyone else's.

"These latkes don't taste soft and light," one of the children said.

"And they don't taste like clouds," another added.

"Some secret recipe," Berel told Yentel after all the latkes were eaten. "They taste just like ours."

"Well," Yentel said, "this just proves that no matter how you make them, latkes always taste the same."

Malke's Latkes

Many would agree that the best part of Hanukkah is the potato latkes. In fact, some families even have latke-eating contests! Potato latke recipes have been passed down from generation to generation. Potato latkes are fried in oil as a remembrance of the oil that burned in the Temple for eight days and nights.

Makes about 20 latkes

What You Need: Ingredients

5 medium potatoes, peeled

3 tablespoons flour

vegetable oil for frying

2 large eggs

1 teaspoon salt

dash of pepper

1 tablespoon lemon juice

1 tablespoon parsley flakes

6 scallions, chopped (Use only the light green part of the scallion, not the dark green part.)

sour cream or applesauce

Utensils

grater

egg beater

large bowl
medium bowl

vegetable peeler

knife

strainer or sieve

frying pan

slotted pancake turner

measuring spoons

What You Do:
You'll have to use a knife and the stove for this recipe, so make sure a grown-up is there to help you.

1. Grate the peeled potatoes into the large bowl. Be careful not to cut your fingers.

2. Place the grated potatoes in a sieve in the sink and press out as much liquid as possible. Then put the potatoes back into the bowl.

3. Beat the eggs in the medium bowl. Add them to the grated potatoes in the large bowl.

4. Add the remaining ingredients.

5. Heat ½ inch of oil in the frying pan.

6. Drop 1 tablespoon of the mixture into the oil for each latke. Flatten the mixture and allow it to brown on each side, turning once with the slotted pancake turner. Cook several latkes at once — as many as the pan will hold.

7. Remove the latkes from the frying pan with the slotted pancake turner. Place them on paper towels to drain.

8. Serve with sour cream or applesauce.

Spin, Little Dreidels

Follow the instructions below each line and you'll have a great time!

Spin, little dreidels,
go, go, go.
Turn.

Spin, little dreidels,
now, go slow.
Turn slowly.

Spin, little dreidels,
jump so high.
Jump.

Spin, little dreidels,
reach for the sky.
Stretch arms upward.

Spin, little dreidels,
touch your nose.
Touch nose.

Spin, little dreidels,
stand on your toes.
Stand on toes.

Spin, little dreidels,
take a hop.
Hop on one foot.

Spin, little dreidels,
don't you stop.
Keep hopping.

Spin, little dreidels,
spin around.
Turn.

Spin, little dreidels,
drop to the ground.
Sit down.

44

My Dreidel

I have a lit-tle drei-del, I made it out of clay; And

when it's dry and read-y Then drei-del I shall play. O

drei-del, drei-del, drei-del, I made it out of clay; O

drei-del, drei-del, drei-del, Now drei-del I shall play.

2. It has a lovely body
   With legs so short and thin;
   And when it is all tired,
   It drops and then I win.

   Oh, dreidel, dreidel, dreidel,
   With legs so short and thin;
   Oh, dreidel, dreidel, dreidel,
   It drops and then I win.

3. My dreidel's always playful,
   It loves to dance and spin;
   A happy game of dreidel —
   Come play, now let's begin.

   Oh, dreidel, dreidel, dreidel,
   It loves to dance and spin;
   Oh, dreidel, dreidel, dreidel,
   Come play, now let's begin.

Let's Play Dreidel

Hanukkah wouldn't be Hanukkah without a dreidel. The Hebrew letters on the sides of the dreidel stand for the first letters in the Hebrew sentence *Nes gadol hayah sham*, which means "A great miracle happened there." The miracle was the reclaiming of the Temple of Jerusalem.

Dreidel is an easy game to learn. Just read this rhyme and before you know it, you'll be playing!

Nun, gimel, heh, and *shin*,
See the wooden dreidel spin.
Nes gadol hayah sham,
If I'm lucky I will win!

I play with my new dreidel
upon the shiny floor.
I ask some friends to play with me —
we must have two or more.

I give the players pennies —
the same amount to each.
We sit down in a circle,
the pennies within reach.

Each player puts a penny
in the proper spot.
The middle of the circle
is what we call the "pot."

Next I take the dreidel
and spin it round and round.
Which letter does it land on?
What fortune have I found?

I read the letter facing up —
it tells me how to play.
The letters are in Hebrew,
and here is what they say:

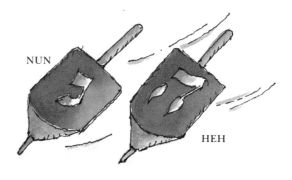

Nun means I do nothing —
I neither give nor take.
Heh means I take half the pot —
what a lucky break!

Gimel means I take it all.
It looks as if I'll win!
But I must put a penny back
when it lands on *shin*.

One thing to remember
before the players spin:
If the pot is empty,
each player puts one in.

We go around the circle —
it's lots and lots of fun,
till one has all the pennies.
Then the game is done!

Nun, *gimel*, *heh*, and *shin*,
See the wooden dreidel spin.
Nes gadol hayah sham,
If I'm lucky I will win!

And while we are playing.
The candles are burning low.
One for each night,
They shed a sweet light
To remind us of days long ago.

A *Hanukkah Memory by Shari Lewis*

The year I was thirteen, on the night before Hanukkah, Papa put me on a train heading for Johnstown, Pennsylvania. At first, Mama and Papa were worried about me traveling all the way from New York City by myself, but in the end they let me go. I was alone, and excited to be heading to my first out-of-town show for the Jewish Center Lecture Bureau. My suitcase contained a red dress, red shoes, and a big ventriloquist's dummy (not Lamb Chop, for she wasn't born yet!). I also had an hour's worth of Jewish-content magic tricks: a candle that magically became *eight* candles (to honor the story of Judah Macabee in the Temple), a sheet of newspaper which, when ripped, miraculously restored itself in the shape of a Jewish star, and so on.

I had boarded the train late that evening and delightedly went to sleep in my upper berth. At 6:00 A.M., I awakened and was startled to see a black sky above, white snow below, and huge flames in between. These were the foundries of Johnstown, Pennsylvania.

The rabbi who had invited me to perform at his Jewish Center met the train and took me to his home, where I spent the day playing with his little son. The boy was bright and funny, and his company kept me from any thoughts of stage fright. Late that afternoon, I did my Hanukkah show for an audience full of Jewish children.

After the show, the rabbi put me back on the train, and Papa met me at the station in New York. From the moment I saw him I rattled on about my wonderful trip to Johnstown. I told him this was the way I wanted to spend *every* Hanukkah, and for years and years, that's just what happened. Until my late teens, when I got my first TV series, my holidays were spent on the road.

But the highlight of this first professional holiday journey did not reveal itself until decades later.

One day, I arrived at the publishing house that distributed my books, and was told that I had a new editor. When I went in to meet him, I extended my hand, but instead of a handshake I got a hug.

"Oh, you know me, Shari," he said, grinning. "Once upon a time, when you went to Johnstown, Pennsylvania, to do a Hanukkah show, you came to my house. I was the rabbi's son!"

Light the Festive Candles
Aileen Fisher

Light the first of eight tonight —
the farthest candle to the right.

Light the first and second, too,
when tomorrow's day is through.

Then light three, and then light four —
every dusk one candle more

Till all eight burn bright and high,
honoring a day gone by

When the Temple was restored,
rescued from the Syrian lord,

And an eight-day feast proclaimed —
The Festival of Lights — well named

To celebrate the joyous day
when we regained the right to pray
to our one God in our own way.

The Two Miracles of Hanukkah

by Charlotte Herman

Outside it was dark. Inside, the house was filled with the bright lights of Hanukkah.

Yonatan and his grandfather had just finished lighting the eighth candle. Now eight candles in a row stood like little soldiers in the small silver menorah. Watching over them was the ninth candle — the *shammash*.

"I can't stop staring at the flames," said Yonatan.

"That's because those flames represent a two-thousand-year-old miracle," said his grandfather. "Or should I say *two* miracles?"

"Two miracles?" Yonatan asked. "What were they?"

"Come sit with me and I'll tell you."

Together they sat down in a big armchair and gazed at the dancing flames on the windowsill.

"Many, many years ago," Yonatan's grandfather began, "the land of Israel — it was called Judea then — was ruled by King Antiochus of Syria. Antiochus was an evil man. He wouldn't allow the Jews to worship God anymore. 'From now on,' he ordered, 'you will worship our gods.'

"Antiochus brought his idols into the Holy Temple in Jerusalem, which belonged to the Jews. For years the Jews had celebrated Sabbath and festivals in the Temple, but Antiochus put a stop to that. He and his soldiers sacrificed pigs at the altar and let animals run wild. They robbed the Temple of its golden menorah and the gold and silver cups and bowls and crowns. 'Anyone who disobeys me will be killed!' he said."

"But they didn't obey, did they, Grandpa?"

"Some did, but most didn't," his grandfather said. "There was an old man, Mattathias, who wouldn't obey. He and his sons fled into the hills to form an army. His strongest son, Judah, became the leader."

"Judah Maccabee," said Yonatan.

"Yes, Judah the Maccabee — better known as 'the hammer' because he struck mighty blows at his enemies. Soon more men joined the small army — farmers and sheep herders, merchants and teachers. There wasn't a soldier among them.

"But Judah taught them all how to fight, and they had faith in God. No matter how many thousands of soldiers Antiochus sent, and no matter that they came on horses and elephants, the Maccabees won battle after battle. Finally they drove the Syrians out of Jerusalem."

"The first miracle," said Yonatan.

"The first miracle," his grandfather repeated. "And now for the second miracle.

"When the Jews finally came back

to the Temple, they were horrified at what they saw — the Temple was in ruins! Tall weeds were growing in the courtyard and the gates to the Temple were broken. Inside the Temple it was worse.

"The idols that had been sent by Antiochus's soldiers were covered with layer upon layer of dust. But that was nothing compared to the floor, which was covered with blood, ashes, and animal droppings. The place was filthy.

"The Maccabees took the idols outside and smashed them to bits. Then they washed and scrubbed the Temple from top to bottom. They took away the old altar and built a new one out of stones. They polished the marble tiles and made new curtains for the Holy Ark, the wooden cabinet in which the Torah was held. At last they brought in new vessels of silver and gold, and a new golden menorah. The Temple was ready to be rededicated to God.

"Jews came from all over Judea for the celebration. Joy and happiness were felt by everyone. People danced and sang in the streets, and children played in the courtyard.

"When it came time to light the menorah, all they could find was one small jar of pure olive oil. It was enough to last for only one day. This was a problem! The menorah lights were *never* supposed to go out.

"'What will we do?' the people asked each other. 'It will take many days to find more oil.'

"'Have faith,' said Judah Maccabee.

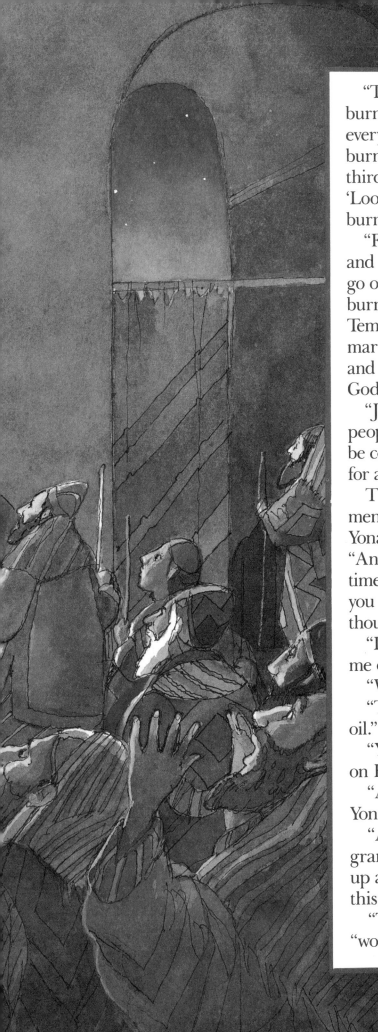

"They lit the menorah, and the oil burned for the first day. And — to everyone's surprise — the oil was still burning on the second day! On the third day people called to each other, 'Look! Three days and the oil still burns. How can this be?'

"Four days went by, then five, six, and seven days. The lights would not go out. For eight days the flames burned strong and bright in the Holy Temple. And for eight days the Jews marveled at the miracle. They danced and celebrated and gave thanks to God.

"Judah Maccabee spoke before the people. 'Let the miracle of these days be celebrated with gladness and joy for all time.'"

The candles in the small silver menorah were burning very low now. Yonatan's grandfather turned to him. "And so, Yonatan," he said, "every time you light the Hanukkah candles, you see these miracles of two thousand years ago."

"Do you know what the oil reminds me of?" Yonatan asked.

"What?" said his grandfather.

"The potato latkes that we fry in oil."

"Yes, that's why we eat potato latkes on Hanukkah," his grandfather said.

"And nothing tastes better!" said Yonatan.

"Ah, what a wonderful idea," his grandfather said. "Why don't we fry up a batch — you peel, I'll fry. And this time I'll try not to burn them."

"That," said Yonatan, smiling, "would be the third miracle."

Maoz Tzur: Rock of Ages

A Hanukkah Memory by Eric A. Kimmel

Going through my grandmother's treasure box is one of my favorite Hanukkah memories. Nana kept the old shoebox in her closet. Every year after lighting the candles she would set the box on the kitchen table. One by one she would show us the objects inside. Each one had a story.

There was a medal that the emperor of Austria gave to my great-grandfather. My great-grandfather went into the Austrian army in 1856 and served for eight years. Because he was the best-looking soldier in the regiment, the general made him his orderly. My great-grandfather held the general's horse in battle when the bullets flew around. Once the general gave him an important message for the emperor. Great-grandfather rode for two days to deliver it. That's how he earned the medal.

There was also an old letter written in faded Hebrew letters. It was from my great-great-uncle Isaac. When he was eighty years old he decided he wanted to die in Jerusalem. Isaac said good-bye and set out for the Holy Land on foot. One year later his family received this letter from him, mailed from Jerusalem. "I have come to the end of my journey," he wrote. "I am at peace." That was the last they heard from him. He is buried on the Mount of Olives.

My favorite treasure was Nana's brass dreidel. For some reason it always fell on *gimel*, the winning letter in the dreidel game. That dreidel had been in our family for more than a hundred years, Nana said. And no surprise! Who would part with a winning dreidel?

There were many treasures in that box, but most precious of all are the memories.

Nine Little Candles

Nine little candles — what a sight!
They stand in the menorah and look so bright.

This one said, "I want to sway."
This one said, "I'm melting away."
This one said, "I'm still pretty tall."
This one said, "I'm getting small."
This one said, "I feel like skipping."
This one said, "My wax is dripping."
This one said, "I have no more light."
This one said, "It's the last Hanukkah night."

The *shammash* said with a shout,
"I'll be the last candle to go out!"

"For eight long days, we did burn.
We'll see you next Hanukkah when we return."

Sylvia Rouss

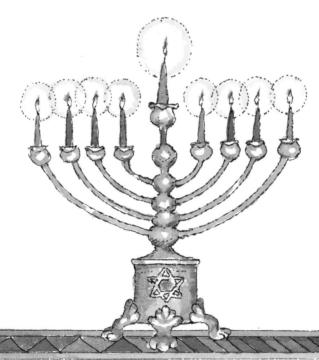

Acknowledgments

Every effort has been made to trace the ownership of all copyrighted materials and to secure the necessary permissions to reprint these selections. If any question arises as to the use of any material, the editor and the publisher, while expressing regret for any inadvertent error, will make the necessary correction in future printings.

Grateful acknowledgment is made to the following for permission to reprint copyrighted material: GRM ASSOCIATES, INC., agents for Ralph Taylor for "A Festival of Lights" by Sydney Taylor from *More All-of-a-Kind Family*. Copyright © 1954 by Follett Publishing Co., copyright renewed 1982 by Ralph Taylor. HARPERCOLLINS PUBLISHERS for "Light the Festive Candles" by Aileen Fisher from *Skip Around the Year* by Aileen Fisher. Copyright © 1967. KAR-BEN COPIES, INC., for *Malke's Secret Recipe, A Chanukah Story* by David A. Adler. Copyright © 1989 by David A. Adler. MARIAN REINER for "The Lights of Chanukah," by Myra Cohn Livingston. Copyright © 1982 by Myra Cohn Livingston. This poem originally appeared in *Cricket* magazine. THE UAHC PRESS for "Five Little Pieces of Hanukkah Gelt," "Nine Little Candles," and "Spin, Little Dreidels" from *Fun with Jewish Holiday Rhymes* by Sylvia Rouss. Copyright © 1992 The UAHC Press. WOMEN'S LEAGUE OF CONSERVATIVE JUDAISM for "What's in My Pocket?" by Sadie Rose Weilerstein. Copyright © 1976.

Our special thanks to David A. Adler, Eric A. Kimmel, Shari Lewis, and Jack Prelutsky for sharing their Hanukkah memories.